Reinah   1981

About Nice

	DATE DUE		
MAY 30 1981	MAR. 1 2 1983	APR. 2 0 1991	
		JUN. 2 2 1991	
JUN. 6 - 1981			
JUL. 2 5 1981	AUG 8 1983	NOV. 2 8 1992	
NOV. 2 8 1981	OCT. 4 1984		
DEC. 1 9 1981	NOV. 2 6 1984		
MAY 3 1982	MAY 3 1 1986		
JUL. 8 1982	JUN. 1 1 1987		
N. 29	SEP. 1 0 1987		
JAN. 3 - 1983	OCT. 1 3 1990		
JAN. 1 8 1983	NOV. 1 7 1990		

THIS

SWEET PICKLES

BOOK
BELONGS TO

In the Town of Sweet Pickles, the animals get
into and out of pickles because of their all too
human personality traits.

Each of the books in the *Sweet Pickles* series
is about a different pickle.

This story is about what nice is ... and isn't.

Library of Congress Cataloging in Publication Data

Reinach, Jacquelyn.
    What's so great about nice?
    (Sweet Pickles series)
    SUMMARY: Jealous Jackal learns why Loving
Lion receives so many valentines.
    [1. St. Valentine's Day — Fiction.   2. Animals —
Fiction]   I. Hefter, Richard.   II. Title.
III. Series.
PZ7.R2747Wg   [E]   80-21438
ISBN 0-937524-02-6

Published by Euphrosyne, Inc.

Sweet Pickles is the registered trademark of
Perle/Reinach/Hefter

Printed in the United States of America

Weekly Reader Books' Edition

Weekly Reader Books presents

WHAT'S SO GREAT ABOUT NICE?

Written by Jacquelyn Reinach
Illustrated by Richard Hefter
Edited by Ruth Lerner Perle

Euphrosyne Incorporated

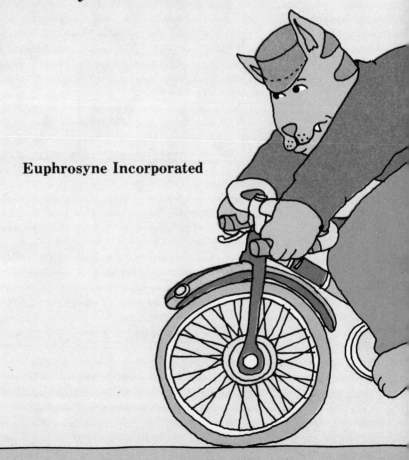

It was Valentine's Day in the Town of Sweet Pickles.
Loving Lion's mailbox was stuffed full of valentines.
Lion sat in his front yard opening the cards and
smiling very big smiles.

Just then, Jealous Jackal rode by on his bicycle. Doubtful Dog was riding with him.

Jackal saw Lion's big pile of valentines. "That's not fair!" cried Jackal. "Lion has all those valentines and I only got one!"

"I bet you sent that one to yourself!" muttered Dog.

"I did not!" cried Jackal. "Positive Pig sent it to me.
I'll show you!"

"Pig sends valentines to *everybody* ... even me!"
said Dog.

"It's just not fair!" whined Jackal. "Why should Lion get more valentines than I do?"

"Because," said Dog, "Lion is nice to everybody and you're not!"

Jackal swerved his bicycle into the curb. "Okay, Dog," he growled. "End of the road! Ride's over!" He dumped Dog off the bike. Dog went SPLAT into a big puddle of water.

"See, I was right!" shouted Dog. "You are *not* nice!"

Jackal pedalled to the gas station and went to work. "Nice!" he muttered as he unlocked the gas pumps. "What's so great about nice?"

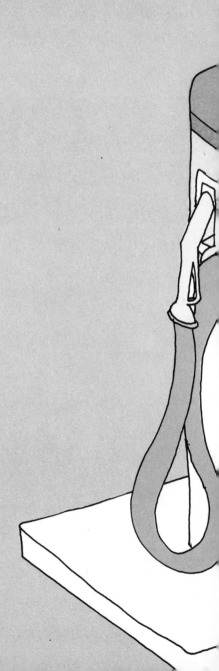

Clever Camel pulled up in her truck. "Hi, Jackal!" she called. "Give me some gas as fast as you can. Lion's roof needs fixing and he's much too nice to be kept waiting!"

"Nice! Nice!" grumbled Jackal. "That's all I ever hear. What's so nice about Lion anyway?"

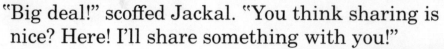

"Well," smiled Camel, "Lion always shares things."
"Big deal!" scoffed Jackal. "You think sharing is
nice? Here! I'll share something with you!"

Jackal unwrapped a stick of gum. He stuck the whole piece in his mouth and handed the wrapper to Camel.

"See!" he giggled. "I'm sharing. I get the gum and you get the nice wrapper!"

"Verrry funny!" said Camel. "That's not sharing. And that's not nice!"

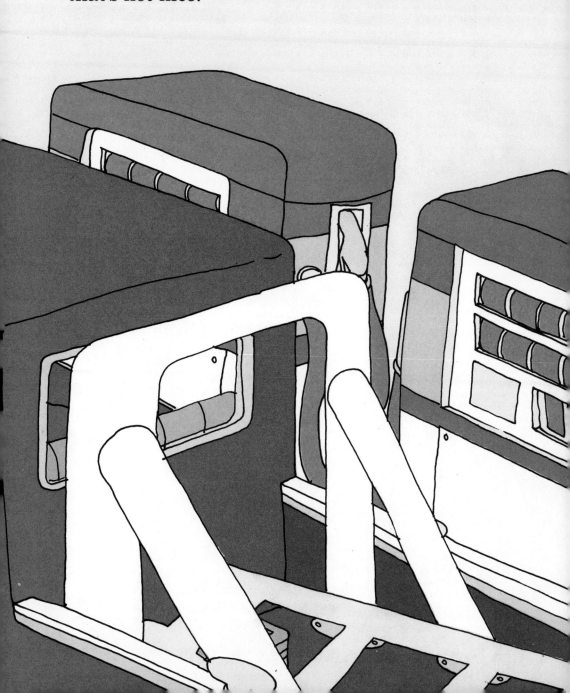

Just then there were loud honks at the car wash around the side of the gas station. It was Responsible Rabbit, looking at his watch.

"Good morning, Jackal," smiled Rabbit. "Can you wash my car? I'm taking Lion for a ride today and I want the car to be clean."

"You're pretty nice to Lion," said Jackal. He gave Rabbit's tires a big kick.

"Of course!" said Rabbit. "Lion's a really nice guy!"

"Nice! Nice! What's so nice about Lion anyway?" grumbled Jackal.

"Well for one thing," said Rabbit, "Lion always helps you. He carries your packages...he waters your flowers...he brings little presents..."

Jackal scratched his ear. "Okay," he grinned. "I'm going to help you, Rabbit, right now!"

"Oh, my!" smiled Rabbit. "How are you going to help?"

"I'm going to save you some money," said Jackal.
"I'm not going to wash your car today!"
"That's a big help!" cried Rabbit. "Thanks a lot!"
Rabbit stepped on the gas and drove off.

All day long, Jackal grumbled and glowered. "Nice! Nice! What's so great about nice?"

In the evening, Jackal closed the gas station and pedalled home.

As he passed Lion's house, he saw all the valentines still on the grass.

Jackal gnashed his teeth and grinned. "I'll show Mister Nice Guy Lion!" he sneered. "I'll take his cards and then they'll be *mine*!"

Jackal jumped off his bike and grabbed Lion's valentines.

Suddenly, the lights went on. Jackal froze. Lion stood in the doorway.

"Good evening, Jackal," smiled Lion. "I see you've picked up all my cards for me. How very nice of you. How very nice indeed!"

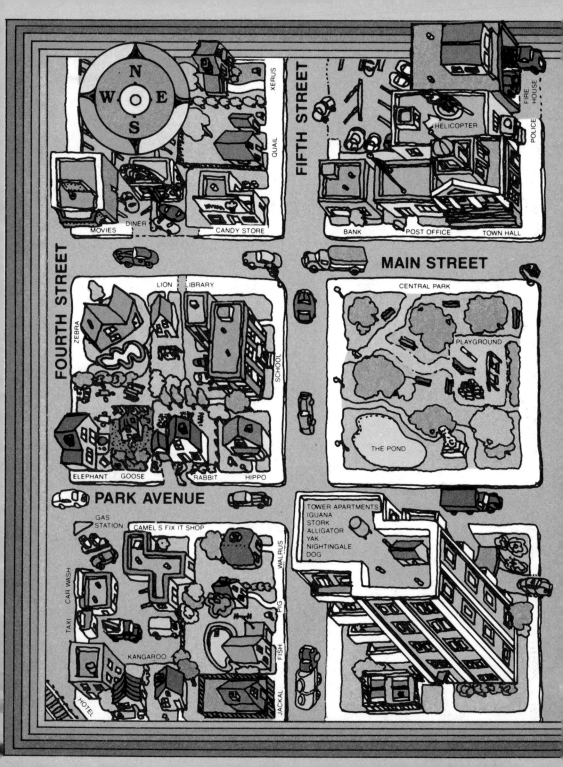